# JUGGLE

Written by Nathan Smith
Illustrated by Aliénor de La Chapelle

The story starts they way many stories do.
A man outside in the storm exposing
himself to the wrath of whatever concept
of God the reader happens to believe in.
He is crying in anguish, letting the storm
obscure his emotions, and he is juggling.
He cries. He juggles. He drops one of the
batons in a muddy puddle and drops to his
knees—continuing to juggle the remaining
two batons. He cries harder and—as if he is
symbiotic with the very universe—the sky
rains harder too. Man and nature in perfect
unison as two hot pink batons dance against
the night sky.

Perhaps we should take another step back
to a story even more familiar. It is two
weeks previous and the man who would be
juggler has yet to connect with the world
he obliquely walks through. He has a name.
A very human name. Let's call him Pierre.
He has a normal life. He has a normal job
and a normal wife. He has two and a half
very normal children and a dog he walks on
Sunday afternoons.

Today is one such Sunday afternoon and he is walking his dog down a country path whilst pushing his half-child in a specially adapted wheelbarrow. The half-child screams out in an agonised voice and he wonders what the other half might be.

Suddenly, the dog starts barking in a soft baritone at another dog. This dog is returning from the country path and is being walked by another rather normal man who is pushing what Pierre can only assume is the other half of his half-child. Both half-children also sense this and escape from their specially adapted wheelbarrows, mounting their respective dogs, and riding down the country path at a suitably quick canter.

Pierre nods at the other man and they both agree to wait at the pub for the half-children to return. They each take half a pint of the cheapest ale and share a packet of dry roasted peanuts in a testimony to the austerity in which they have lived their lives. Pierre tells the man how he works in an office sending emails to customers who have bought something that was made in Taiwan and that he has two other children that are complete in the essence of their child-ness.

He goes to show the man a photo of them all on his phone but soon realises that no such photo exists as his children keep blinking and so he has to keep deleting every photo he takes. Instead, he asks about the man and what type of normal existence he leads.

The man says his name is Jean and that
he also has two other children that have
not disappeared down a country path. He
apologises and says he would show a photo
but his children keep winking and it would
feel inflammatory to pirates to keep such
photos on his phone. He says he works in an
office answering phone calls from customers
who are wanting to return products the
never truly bought. He raises his half-pint in
a toast to their missing half-children and the
barman joins in. One of the regulars lets out
a moan of approval too.

At this point, the two half-children return having taken the opportunity to merge into a complete child whose soul was finally capable to being damned. With renewed confidence, the two mouths of the complete child open and chant in unison. In one of their four hands they hold the head of the hardest clown in the village and the two dogs that had so gallantly carried them away now lapped at the sparkling blood that dripped from his near-empty clown-y arteries.

To put this rather shocking event into context, it is important to understand that Bobo was (or had been) a menace. Some readers of a certain generation may remember his rampages that dominated the front pages of the red tops for a good number of years. Indeed, the author (the one who writes this) lost an uncle to Bobo who, in a fit of rage over unpaid gambling debts, bludgeoned him to death with a balloon animal. No amount of handkerchiefs could wipe away the blood or the tears.

Anyhow, Pierre and Jean now sit in a pub with two half-empty half-pints and a singular child formed from the composite of their two previous half-children. This singular entity collectively holds the face-painted head of the most violent man seen this side of Milton Keynes. It is, to put it mildly, not an ideal situation.

Custody-agreements are quickly drawn and
shallow graves quickly dug. The moaning
regular offers up a mumbled prayer and
unsolicited legal advice and Pierre returns
to his wife sans half-child but with a promise
that he gets every other weekend and school
holidays with the newly complete child. On
the way, he throws his bloodstained dog in
the river to hide the evidence but it swims to
the other side.

His wife is understandably distraught.
His two other complete children are less
understandably less distraught and Pierre
blames the emotionally-complex situations in
video games for desensitising them. He offers
his wife a half-eaten sandwich in the shape
of an apology but quickly finds himself on the
other side of the house to which he usually
resides with a specially-adapted empty
wheelbarrow, a dog collar, and the rest of his
fancy-dress priest outfit that his wife found
distasteful in the wake of Vatican II.

Accident becoming opportunity, Pierre dresses himself in the outfit and squats in the abandoned parish church. "Huzzah for the decline of Christianity!", he thinks as beds down between the pews. It is cold and damp but the abandoned pillows that the old ladies used to kneel on to pray form an excellent makeshift bed. He thinks of the life he has lost and slowly starts to weep.
A raindrop falls on graveyard pigeon.

Pierre awakes to find himself surrounded by lesser clowns in fedoras. "Blood for blood" they say, "sparkle for sparkle" - and he is quickly press-ganged to join them. They force him into a reasonably sized car and Pierre is offered some chewing gum. He accepts and is greeted with an electric shock. He is then given some chewing gum by a different clown as they laugh in a honking type of way.

Minutes turn to hours turn to days turn
to about two-weeks and Pierre no longer
recognises himself. His weekend with his
new complete child is split in half with his
wife and he takes the child shopping whilst
supervised by Giggles. They all share a
milkshake and fight over the single straw.
At the end of the day he hands the complete
child to his wife(?) and he returns to the
dirty clown work that has become his
everyday. He sells sugar-free candyfloss to
uneducated children and pet insurance to
their parents. Each night tears flow from him
like water from a balloon and grey clouds
gather above the circus tent. He rises early
each day to reapply his make-up. He thinks
of his wife and the one child he actually likes.
He decides to make a change.

Pierre stays awake one night and waits for all the other clowns to collapse in a giant clown pile. He decides on a grand romantic gesture and picks the circus trick he knows best.

He frees the elephants and kicks the small weird one with giant ears. He becomes a better man. He runs to his wife like mascara runs down a sad clown's face.

Less exhausted than he expected to be,
Pierre gets to his house his wife's house. She
is there. She is in the arms of Jean as their
newly complete child stands and claps and
the two bloodstained dogs bark at each other,
one slightly wetter than the other. Giggles
is also there holding two milkshakes with
an appropriate amount of straws. They are
all wearing tasteless priest outfits (even the
dogs).

Distraught, Pierre reflects on the mistakes
he has made in life. Reaching the end of
his story, he reaches into the specially
wheelbarrow and grabs the batons signed
with his wife's name and those of his two
children born complete.
The heavens open and crash down upon him.
He juggles and he cries and he lets the rain
wash away his face. His sins still remain.